Enchanted Tree
Vanity Finds No Beauty

Davy Liu

KENDU

Written and illustrated
by Davy Liu

Contributing Author: Dr. Mark Arvidson

Special thanks to my wife, Joan, my forever soul mate and an angel sent from God; Dr. Mark Arvidson; Ben Chambers; Sophie Tsai; Betsy Chiu; CBC church family; Biola University; and the friends that support and pray for Kendu Films.

D.L.

© 2012 by Kendu Films LLC. All rights reserved.

Published in the United States by Kendu Films, LLC.
27068 La Paz Road, #543, Aliso Viejo, CA 92656
www.kendufilms.com

Unless otherwise indicated, all Scriptures are taken from the Holy Bible, New International Version, Copyright 1973, 1978, 1984 by the International Bible Society. Used by permission of Zondervan Publishing House. The "NIV" and "New International Version" trademarks are registered in the United States Patent and Trademark Office by International Bible Society.

ISBN 978-0-982505083

Printed in Korea

For the Creator

Long ago, there was an Enchanted Paradise, beautifully perfect in every way. Yet, this was no fairytale. It was real!

Of the many flowers and fruit trees, one tree stood apart from the rest, with rare fruit unlike any other.

In fact, it was rumored that this fruit revealed a mysterious power over whoever dared to taste it.

Enchanted Tree

*E*ach creature that lived in this paradise had a unique personality.

Miki was a graceful tomboy swinging in trees with her long, beautiful tail.

Reina – a tall, feathered beauty – thought she was a queen, while Leona's spotted coat was always nicely groomed.

Then, there was shy Octavia with her funny-shaped mouth. She didn't feel quite as pretty as the others.

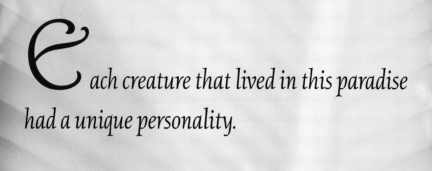

Octavia was jealous of the other creatures. After all, they were beautiful and often made fun that Octavia was odd.

Suddenly, their teasing was interrupted by the outstretched wings of a majestic Phoenix.

The silent creatures stared in amazement.

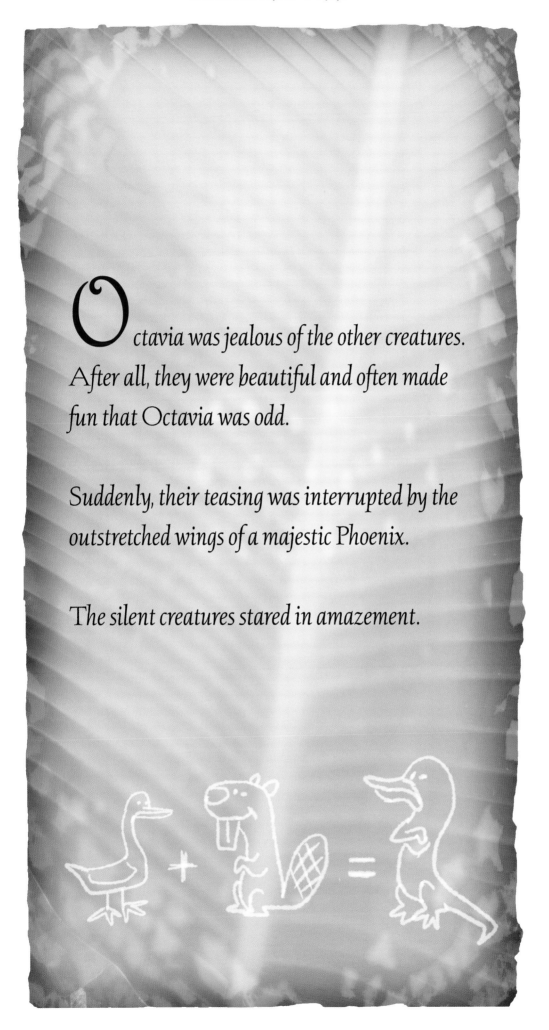

The proud Phoenix boasted of a special fruit that gave her such beauty and a very special ability.

She could transform herself to be whatever she wanted to be.

The creatures listened closely to the Phoenix.

She began to describe the Enchanted Tree that sat in the center of Paradise Garden.

She explained that eating the tree's fruit would give them all the power, beauty and knowledge that they desired.

H

er words were convincing.

The creatures began to crave the fruit and the great power that it promised, but none more than Octavia.

Then, they heard a voice.

The voice belonged to Gabe, a noble gazelle who stood in the garden.

He told them that eating the fruit from the Enchanted Tree would surely bring them the bitter taste of death.

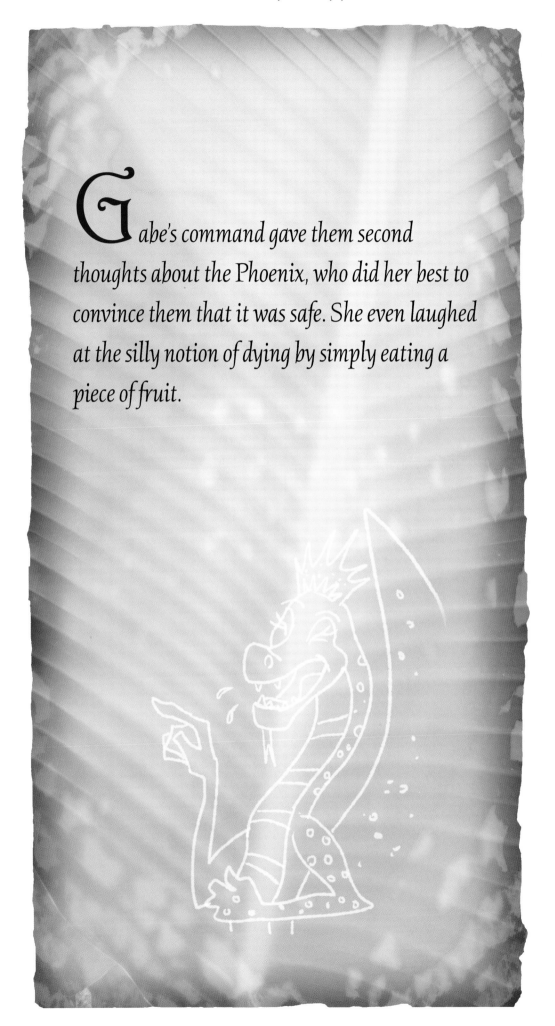

Gabe's command gave them second thoughts about the Phoenix, who did her best to convince them that it was safe. She even laughed at the silly notion of dying by simply eating a piece of fruit.

Octavia wanted the fruit more than any of the other creatures. She had always dreamed of being beautiful.

Now, the Phoenix offered her fruit from the Enchanted Tree that could make her dream come true.

The offer was interrupted by the sound of "chewing"! Octavia was worried that another creature had gotten to the magical fruit before she did.

Enchanted Tree

The creatures got an unexpected surprise, especially the Phoenix, when a mysterious stranger was walking among the trees.

As he walked, the odd creature went from tree to tree tasting all of the fruit that he could eat. However, the Enchanted Tree still remained untouched.

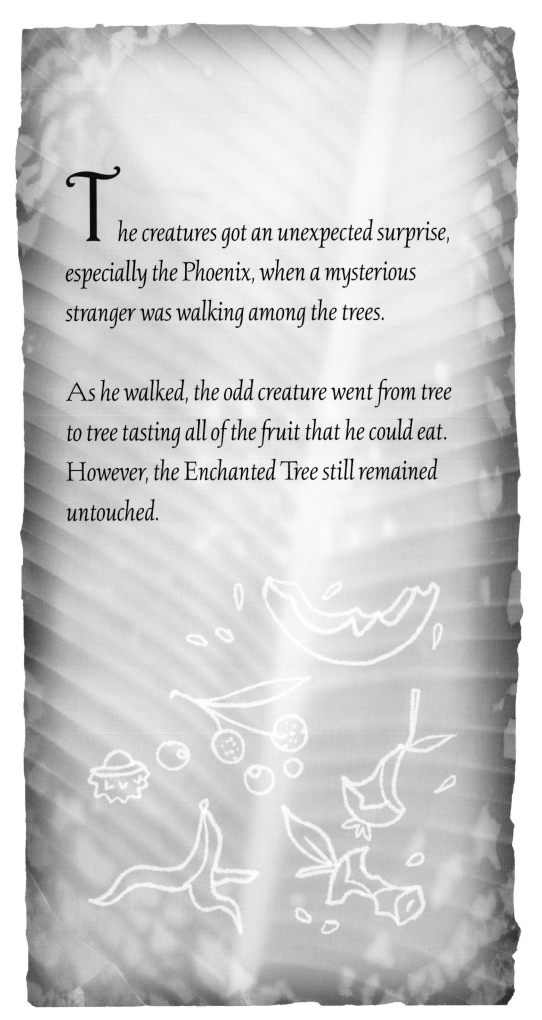

Enchanted Tree

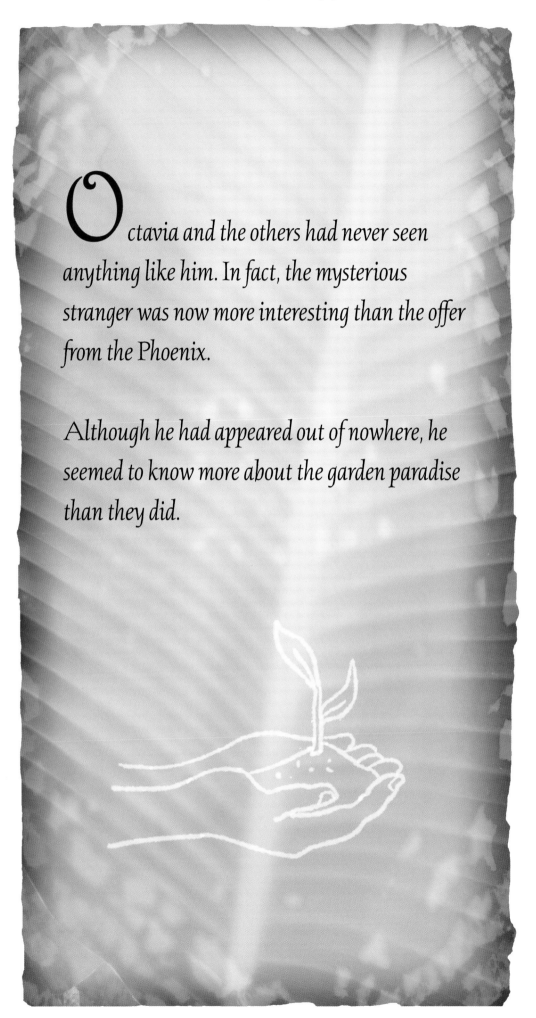

Octavia and the others had never seen anything like him. In fact, the mysterious stranger was now more interesting than the offer from the Phoenix.

Although he had appeared out of nowhere, he seemed to know more about the garden paradise than they did.

They offered him fruit. In return, he gave them the name, ANIMALS.

Then, starting with Octavia, he gave every animal their own identity.

The platypus, monkey, leopard and crane each had a name of their own – none more important than the other.

This greatly upset the Phoenix, because she knew that in order to get even one animal to eat the mysterious fruit, she would have to turn away the friendly, new stranger.

The animals enjoyed the new stranger so much that they and Octavia trusted him as their leader. They also noticed that he was unhappy being alone. So each animal competed to become his helpmate.

Miki swung from the trees with her long tail, hoping to be chosen, but she wasn't a match. Even Reina, with her feathery crown and Leona, with her spotted coat were not good matches. Octavia slapped her tail on the ground, but she still was not a suitable helpmate.

The Phoenix spied as, one by one, the creatures tried to take away their new friend's loneliness.

Then, later that night, something amazing happened!

Enchanted Tree

The Phoenix continued to spy as the stranger fell into a deep sleep.

In a flash of light, another Two-feeter appeared, as if from out of his flesh, while he slept.

She was beautiful and perfectly suited to be his helpmate.

Enchanted Tree

At first the animals were happy that their leader had a new helpmate, but things soon began to change. The animals noticed that the new helpmate was now more important to their leader than they were. He spent less time with them than before.

Their sadness turned to jealousy, and then to anger.

They wanted things to return to the way they were.

Enchanted Tree

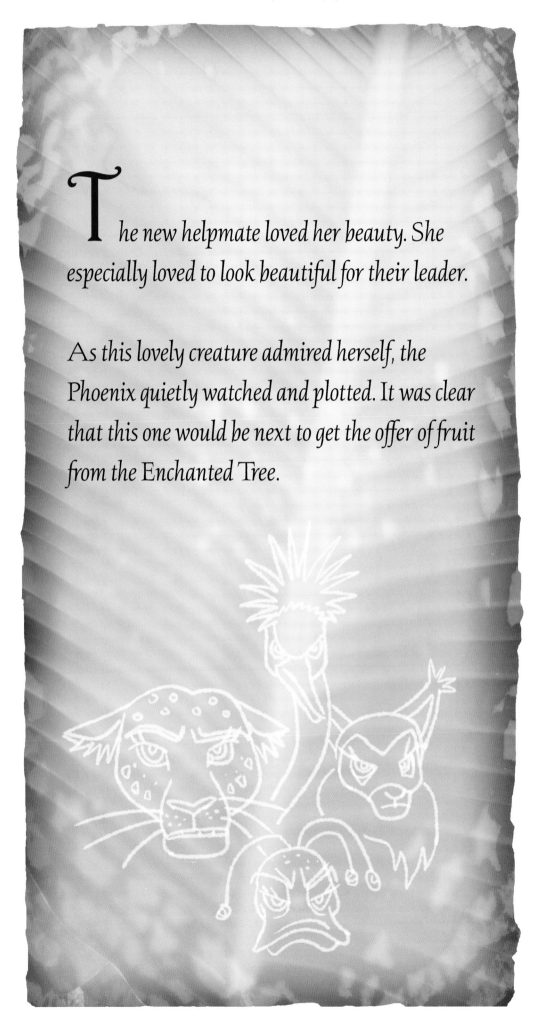

The new helpmate loved her beauty. She
especially loved to look beautiful for their leader.

As this lovely creature admired herself, the
Phoenix quietly watched and plotted. It was clear
that this one would be next to get the offer of fruit
from the Enchanted Tree.

The Phoenix convinced Octavia to lure the helpmate to the Enchanted Tree to prove that Gabe's warning of death was untrue. The other animals followed as Octavia led her to the center of the Paradise Garden, and there it was!

The Enchanted Tree filled them all with wonder. It was even better than the Phoenix had described it. Now, she was coiled around it waiting in disguise for the helpmate to take a closer look.

Enchanted Tree

The helpmate moved closer toward the Tree, seeing her own reflection in the shiny fruit. As she stared at her beauty, the twisting Phoenix whispered in her ear to have a taste.

The helpmate paused for a moment, considering the rumors she had heard about dying. The slippery tongue of the Phoenix was quick to tell her otherwise.

She promised the helpmate great power to match her beauty. Quickly, the uncertain Two-feeter grabbed the fruit in her hand.

She took the fruit and ate it. In an instant, she felt that the Two-feeters were better than all the animals in the garden – even better than whoever made the garden.

Then, she took the fruit and gave it to the animals' leader. The animals were surprised that neither of them had died. Especially Octavia, who had hoped to win back their friendship by giving them the powerful fruit.

The helpmate urged the Two-feeter to get rid of the animals so that they could keep the fruit to themselves. Their leader loved his helpmate more than the animals, and even more than his own life.

So, he agreed.

The animals heard of this and became very afraid.

The dark chill of nightfall covered the sky. The Two-feeter leader and his helpmate had no coverings for their shivering bodies.

While the leopard nibbled pieces of fruit left on the ground, his once caring leader approached to steal her fur for warmth. The Leopard quickly showed her angry fangs. The fruit had changed her, too.

The other animals feared for their fur and their lives, turning against one another to survive. The Paradise Garden was no longer a paradise at all.

For the first time, the Two-feeters were alone in the garden. Their home was empty and so were their stomachs.

While walking through the dry land looking for food, they heard footsteps and quickly hid themselves.

They heard a sad voice – Gabe, the Gazelle – asking them what they had done.

As they stepped out, he gazed into their eyes and their hunger turned to shame. They had disobeyed his command.

The Two-feeters were ordered out of the garden, because they had chosen to believe a lie instead of the truth.

The deserted land was an eerie sight to the animals as they crept out from hiding. They found the Phoenix bragging of her plan to become ruler of the garden, once the fruit was eaten.

Only Octavia was sad and ashamed at what she had done.

The Phoenix laughed and sneered as she stretched her neck upward. She tried to return to her former winged beauty, but nothing happened.

She was cursed to remain crawling on her belly, because of her lies.

Enchanted Tree

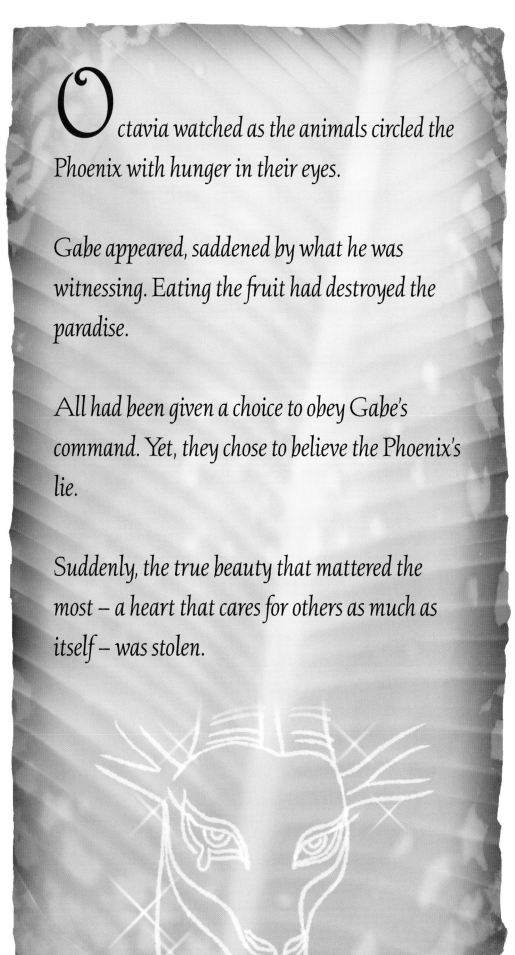

O ctavia watched as the animals circled the Phoenix with hunger in their eyes.

Gabe appeared, saddened by what he was witnessing. Eating the fruit had destroyed the paradise.

All had been given a choice to obey Gabe's command. Yet, they chose to believe the Phoenix's lie.

Suddenly, the true beauty that mattered the most – a heart that cares for others as much as itself – was stolen.

Enchanted Tree

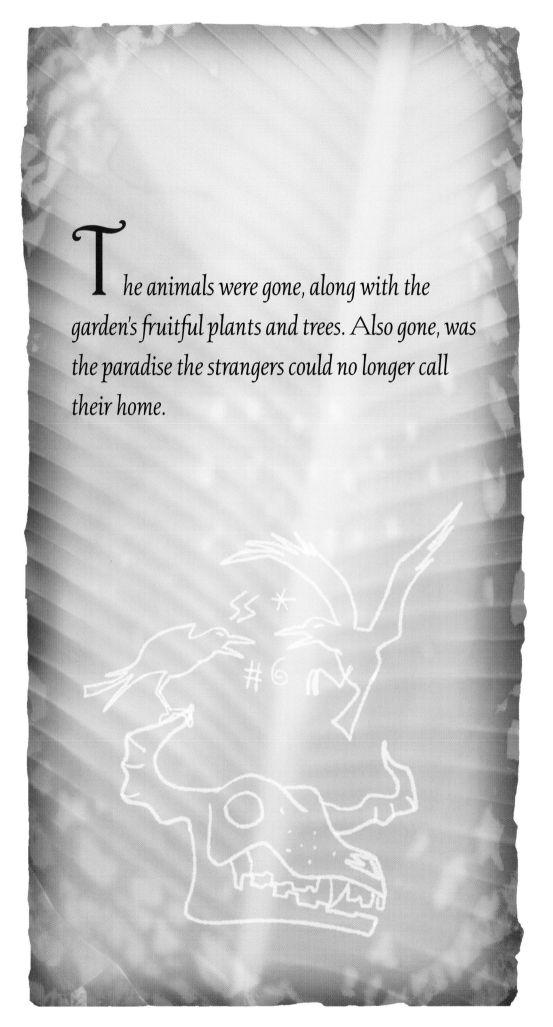

The animals were gone, along with the garden's fruitful plants and trees. Also gone, was the paradise the strangers could no longer call their home.

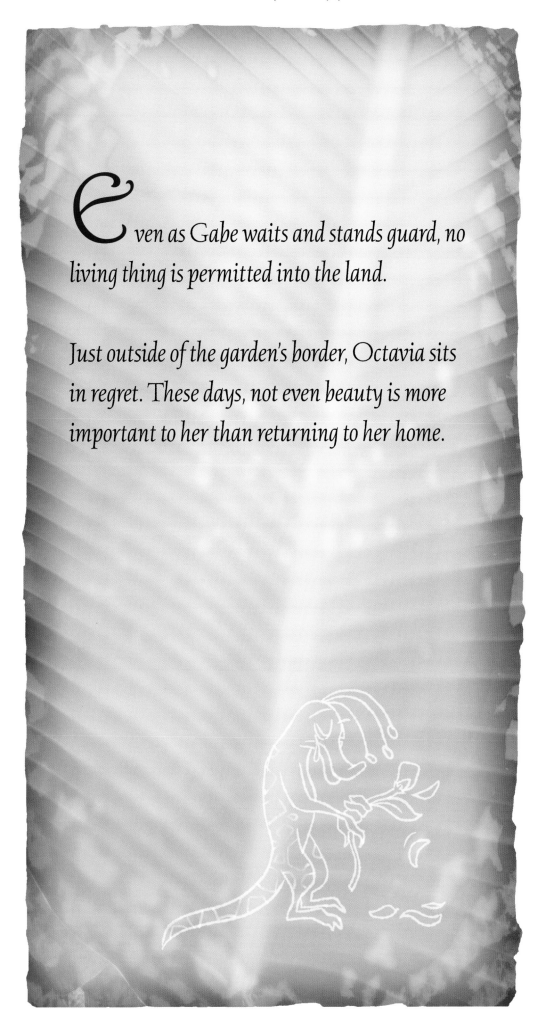

Even as Gabe waits and stands guard, no living thing is permitted into the land.

Just outside of the garden's border, Octavia sits in regret. These days, not even beauty is more important to her than returning to her home.

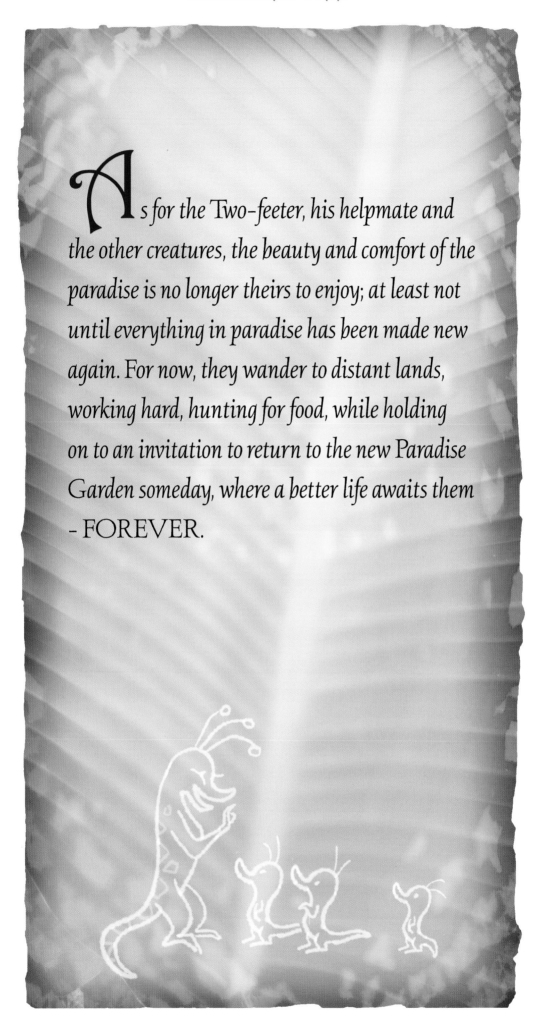

As for the Two-feeter, his helpmate and the other creatures, the beauty and comfort of the paradise is no longer theirs to enjoy; at least not until everything in paradise has been made new again. For now, they wander to distant lands, working hard, hunting for food, while holding on to an invitation to return to the new Paradise Garden someday, where a better life awaits them - FOREVER.

Inspired by the historical events
from the book of Genesis

"Adam and Eve"

*"In the beginning God created the heavens
and the earth......*

*So God created man in his own image, in the
image of God he created him; male and female.*

Moses

*"Blessed are those who wash their robes, that they may
have the right to the tree of life and may go through the
gates into the city."*

Revelation 22:14

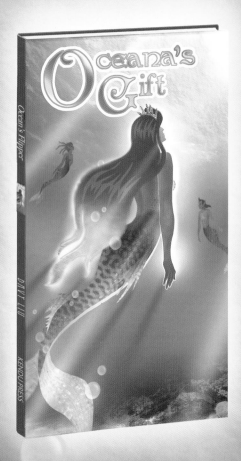